"Hi, I am Captain Pablo.
I am a brave
space race captain."

ICK JR.
The
ACKYARDIGANS
onics Reading Program

Book 9
long *a*

# A Race Through Space

by Sonia Sander

## SCHOLASTIC INC.

New York    Toronto    London    Auckland    Sydney
Mexico City    New Delhi    Hong Kong    Buenos Aires

"Hooray!" called
Captain Pablo.
"Watch out, space racers!
Captain Tyrone and I are
going to win today's
space race."

"Don't be so sure,"
said Captain Uniqua over
her radio. "Captain Austin
and I will chase you.
We will win this race."

"Let's speed away," ordered Captain Pablo. "We can't let them win the space race. We want to take first place."

"Captain Pablo, the spacecraft is starting to shake," said Captain Tyrone. "It can't take this fast pace."

"The spacecraft is
  in bad shape," said
Captain Tyrone.
"We have to make
  a crash landing."

"Hello, brave space racers."
Captain Austin waved.
"We came to save you."
"Hooray!" shouted
Captain Pablo.

"We can win the space
race together!"